Jane Blond
Schoolgirl Superspy

Written by
Jan Burchett and Sara Vogler

Illustrated by David Roberts

CHAPTER ONE

Warning. The story I am about to tell you is top secret. It is for your eyes only. It will self-destruct as soon as you have read it.

First, I want you to take a look at this top secret photograph.

This is the face of Jane Blond, Schoolgirl Superspy.

It is the face of a top secret agent. And not just any old top secret agent.

Jane Blond is number one spy in the famous **N**etwork **O**f **S**nooping **Y**oungsters – **NOSY** for short. And she was hand-picked for the job by none other than The Snout, the big boss of NOSY.

(By the way, the sidekick and handy two-way radio is me, Whiz Kit.)

The story I am about to tell you is a story of danger, daring and dastardly deeds. It is the story of Jane Blond and the Missing Chocolate. (There are school dinners, too, but you can hold your nose when we get to that bit.)

It all happened just last week. It was Friday, it was 08.51 and I was on the phone in the lounge. Jane burst into the room.

'Wake up, Fluffikins!' she shouted in my ear. 'This is an emergency!'

I sprang into action.

Jane snatched up her Schoolgirl Superspy rucksack. She slid out of the window and dived into a bush in the front garden. Making sure the coast was clear, she dropped on to hands and knees and crawled along the pavement. I followed close behind.

She reached a dark doorway, silently turned the door handle and we slipped inside. Were we on a secret mission? No, it was nearly time for school and Jane had run out of chocolate. We were at the sweet shop.

I could see straight away that things were not right at the shop. There were three clues – a puzzled policeman, a sobbing shopkeeper and a row of empty shelves. I knew that Jane's razor-sharp brain would be working at full speed.

She marched past PC Truncheon and over to Mr Sherbet, who was howling into his hanky.

'The name's Blond,' she said. 'Jane Blond. Fifteen bars of Choccomunch, if you please.'

But Mr Sherbet made no attempt to fetch her usual order.

'Oh calamity, Miss Blond,' he wailed. 'I cannot give you your chocolate. A terrible crime has been committed. Someone has stolen all the chocolate bars in my shop – and all the sweets!'

'Then Fluffikins and I must go immediately,' declared Jane, striding towards the door.

I followed her eagerly. Jane Blond, Schoolgirl Superspy, was on the case, and she would need her faithful sidekick.

The name is Whizz Kit

'That's right, Miss Blond,' said PC Truncheon, respectfully removing his helmet. 'You must start your investigations at once.'

'Investigations?' said Jane, turning at the door. 'Not at all. I'm going to find another shop that sells Choccomunch.'

'I'm afraid that won't be possible, Miss Blond,' said PC Truncheon. 'I am informed that this isn't the only sweet shop that has been burgled.'

'You mean …'

'I'm afraid so, Miss. There isn't a sweetie left in all of Snifton.'

Jane gasped.

'So what you're trying to say is, there isn't a sweetie left in all of Snifton!'

PC Truncheon nodded sadly.

'Then there's no time to lose,' declared Jane. 'My Choccomunch is at stake!'

CHAPTER TWO

Jane grabbed me by the scruff of the neck and whisked me off to a quiet corner behind the comics. She twiddled the tag on my collar. My ears twitched, my whiskers pinged and my tail shot up in the air. Nothing strange in that. It's all in a day's work for a cat who is also a handy two-way radio.

'Blond calling, sir,' Jane whispered into my left ear. 'Jane Blond. There's trouble in Snifton. All the Choccomunch has been stolen. Permission to find it, sir.'

'No time, Blond,' came The Snout's answer. 'Something much more important has come up. And NOSY has been picked to investigate. I want you on the case.'

'But, sir …' began Jane, desperately.

The Snout interrupted her. 'Listen carefully, Blond,' he snapped. 'This is top secret. You are to go to Badboys Hall.'

'Badboys Hall, sir?'

'Yes, Blond. Badboys Hall – the new primary school at the edge of town. I smell something fishy going on there. I want you to nose around and then report back to me.'

'But, sir, I should be at school by now.'

'I'll give you a note for your teacher. Safe sniffing.'

'But my Choccomunch, sir …'

It was too late. The Snout had gone. Jane had no choice but to accept her mission. We were off to Badboys Hall.

At 09.34 we were standing in a queue at the town library. You may be wondering why a Schoolgirl Superspy was standing in a library queue when she was on a top secret mission. It was very simple. We needed to see Mr Hooter, the librarian, and it wasn't to have books stamped.

You see, Mr Hooter was not just a librarian. He was also chief gadget maker for NOSY. Jane never went on a mission without picking up a useful tool from him first.

By 09.57 we spotted him in the crime section. Jane and Mr Hooter greeted each other with the top secret NOSY greeting.

..TOP SECRET NOSY GREETING.

CRIME SECTION

'I've been expecting you, Blond,' said Mr Hooter. 'Come with me.'

Checking no one was watching, we followed him to the cookery section. He reached up and pulled out a large book, 'Interesting Ways to Boil Turnips'. He opened it. It wasn't a book about turnips at all. It was a cunningly disguised box and it had an ordinary wooden spoon inside.

'This may look like an ordinary wooden spoon in a cunningly disguised box,' said Mr Hooter proudly, 'but don't be fooled, Blond. It is in fact my latest invention – the Hooter Laserblaster. I'm rather pleased with it, if I say so myself.'

Jane took the spoon and examined it. She thoughtfully tapped the handle three times. Suddenly a beam of dazzling blue light shot out from the end of the spoon and a nearby bookcase exploded – along with two pot plants and a stepladder.

'Yes … well,' said Mr Hooter, flapping a hanky at the smoke. 'I see you've worked out how to use it. Three taps, that's all it takes. Good luck with your mission, Blond. Safe sniffing!'

Jane dropped the spoon into her Schoolgirl Superspy rucksack and strode out of the library.

'For a job like this we need transport,' she said. 'Let me think. It will have to be fast, it will have to be streamlined and no one must notice it.

The Hootercopter? The Hooterscooter?
No, I have just the thing – the
Hootermobile.'

She rummaged in her rucksack
and pulled out a small plastic nose. It
had a green string dangling from one
nostril.

'Stand back, Fluffikins,' she
ordered.

She pulled the string. There was a
rude noise and our transport appeared.

'My Choccomunch will have to
wait,' declared Jane bravely, as she
hopped in. 'We have a mission. We're
off to Badboys Hall.'

CHAPTER THREE

At 10.43 we skidded to a halt outside Badboys Hall Primary School.

    There was a scrap of paper dangling from the school sign. I read it.

    Badboys Hall seemed to be short of dinner ladies. We could use that to our advantage. Meanwhile, the Schoolgirl Superspy had whipped out a magnifying glass and was closely examining the school sign.

'Yes,' she said at last. 'This is Badboys Hall all right. And they seem to be short of dinner ladies. Oh dear, doesn't look like we'll get any school lunch then, Fluffikins. However, the sooner we get in there the better. Now, a place like this will be almost impossible to enter. It's a good job Jane Blond's on the case.'

She zigzagged down the drive, flattened herself against a wall and slithered round the outside of the school. She looked through keyholes, rattled door handles and peered down drains. I hopped on to a window sill to keep a lookout and wait for her. You can't hurry a Schoolgirl Superspy.

At last she had finished her investigations.

'I was right, Fluffikins,' she said. 'I can find no way in.' Then she spotted the open window behind me. 'Ah ha!' she exclaimed. 'I knew there'd be a secret entrance somewhere. Only a top spy would notice that.'

We climbed in and dropped noiselessly to the floor.

We found ourselves in a strange, steamy room. A nasty brown liquid was bubbling in a pot. A massive machine rumbled and squelched. And there was a dreadful pong. Was this the mystery of Badboys Hall? No, we were in the school kitchen. Time to hold your noses.

The place seemed to be deserted.

We set off through the steam. Then, all of a sudden, a huge figure loomed out of the gloom. A fierce-looking woman in a dirty overall towered over us. She bent down and thrust her face into ours.

'Who are you?' she growled.

Quick as a flash, the Schoolgirl Superspy gave a false name.

'The name's Blong,' she said. 'Jane Blong. And we're here to …'

'I know exactly why you're here,' the woman snapped.

Things didn't look good. Jane pulled out her wooden spoon ready for action.

'You're here about the dinner lady jobs. I see you've brought your own wooden spoon ready for action. I'm Mrs Brootle, head dinner lady, and you're just in time. It's nearly twelve o'clock, two of my ladies is off with the chickenpox and there's four hundred and fifty little mouths to feed. And we haven't even started on the afters yet!'

Suddenly she let out a huge roar. 'Mrs Mince! Mrs Suett!'

Two other dinner ladies lurched out of the steam.

'We've got some extra help,' said Mrs Brootle, 'although one of them's a bit small and could do with a shave. So you can get on with your jam roly-poly now, ladies.'

'Yes, Mrs Brootle,' chorused the dinner ladies.

'Okay, Blong,' barked our new boss, 'you'll dish up the bangers and mash. And Shorty – you'll be doing the gravy. Put these overalls on.'

We put our overalls on and at
11.59 we were ready to dish out greasy
sausages and watery gravy.

'This is excellent, Fluffikins,'
whispered Jane. 'Super idea of mine!
No one would know we're not real
dinner ladies.'

At that moment a loudspeaker
above our heads began to crackle. The
dinner ladies stood to attention as a
deep, booming voice filled the air. I
don't mind telling you it made my fur
stand on end.

'CALLING ALL PUPILS. THIS IS PROFESSOR VILLAIN. GOOD WORK ON YOUR ... SPECIAL PROJECT LAST NIGHT. KEEP IT UP.'

'That was our dear headmaster,' explained Mrs Brootle. 'He might be ever so busy but he always sends the little kiddies a message. What are you all standing around for? On with the dinner.'

She lumbered over to the rumbling, squelching machine and turned a tap at the bottom. Piles of disgusting grey mashed potato sploshed into a bowl. She slapped the bowl down in front of Jane. Then suddenly she pointed at Jane's wooden spoon.

'Hang on a minute,' she snarled. 'Give me that!' She snatched the Hooter Laserblaster from Jane's grip and examined it closely. 'Just as I thought!' she muttered.

I gulped. We were in big trouble.

CHAPTER FOUR

The three dinner ladies peered suspiciously at the Hooter Laserblaster.

'This isn't a potato spoon!' hissed Mrs Brootle.

'No, it isn't,' chorused the other dinner ladies.

I looked round for an escape route.

'This is a custard spoon. And I'm having it. No one puts lumps in school custard like I do. Isn't that right, ladies?'

'That's right, Mrs Brootle.'

Jane and I watched as the head dinner lady stirred the custard.

When she had finished she tapped the custard-covered Hooter Laserblaster on the side of the pan. Once. Twice. Three times. There was a dazzling beam of blue light and the pan exploded. Mrs Brootle was covered from head to foot in lumpy custard. She staggered blindly around the kitchen.

I got ready to leap out of the window. But Mrs Brootle just shook herself free of custard and gawped at the mess.

'I must have put too many lumps in again,' she croaked.

Suddenly there was a battle cry of 'Sausages!' and all four hundred and fifty pupils of Badboys Hall Primary School tried to get through the dining room door at once.

'Action stations, ladies!' shouted Mrs Brootle, wiping her face with a mop. 'Here come our little poppets.'

'Bless 'em!' sighed Mrs Mince and Mrs Suett.

I could see straight away there was something wrong with the pupils at this school. There were three clues – they were big, they were mean and there wasn't a child among them. The Snout was right. Something fishy was going on and who better than Jane Blond, Schoolgirl Superspy, to find out exactly what it was.

'What charming children, Fluffikins,' said Jane cheerfully, as she dished up the last jam roly-poly and custard at 12.43 precisely. 'There's obviously nothing fishy going on at Badboys Hall. We'll hang up our overalls, report to The Snout and go back to Snifton to find my Choccomunch.'

Jane picked up her spoon and marched towards the door. I don't know how it happened, but the next minute she was flat on her face in the potato peelings.

'This is no time for rolling about in potato peelings, Blong!' shouted Mrs Brootle. 'You haven't finished yet. You and Shorty have got to take our dear headmaster his special dinner that Mrs Mince has lovingly prepared. Isn't that right, Mrs Mince?'

'That's right, Mrs Brootle.'

'So get on with it! It's down that corridor, turn right and look for the sign, "Professor Villain's office".'

Jane picked up the tray. We were about to set off when the head dinner lady suddenly blocked our path.

'And whatever you do,' she warned, jabbing a podgy finger at us, 'just you stay away from the secret storeroom! It's down the corridor, but you turn left instead and look for the sign that says, "Secret Storeroom – Keep Out Unless You Want Something Nasty To 'appen To You". Hurry up! The Professor doesn't like being kept waiting.'

We made our way along the corridor. I could see that the keen mind of the Schoolgirl Superspy was hard at work, picking up all the clues as we went. And there were plenty.

First there was the maths lesson.

Then there was PE.

And then there was a class doing some science.

At 13.06 we arrived at Professor Villain's office. I could see it was the right place. The sign said, 'Professor Villain's office'. Balancing the tray expertly on one hand, Jane whipped out her magnifying glass. She inspected the nameplate closely.

'Yes, this is Professor Villain's office all right,' she announced at last. She knocked loudly.

'THAT HAD BETTER BE MY DINNER!' boomed a loudspeaker above our heads. 'LEAVE IT THERE AND MAKE YOURSELF SCARCE OR I'LL FEED YOU TO THE CROCODILE!'

CHAPTER FIVE

Professor Villain's voice echoed round us. I was very glad we weren't invited in. But Jane, Schoolgirl Superspy through and through, didn't bat an eyelid.

'Righty-ho, Prof,' she called chirpily, as she put the tray down.

I knew what she was up to now. We were off to look for the secret storeroom – and solve the mystery of Badboys Hall.

'Lead the way, Fluffikins. We're off to Snifton to look for my Choccomunch.'

I led the way. But I suddenly needed to have a good old scratch just outside a huge wooden door with heavy iron hinges. It had a sign on it.

SECRET
P.E. STOREROOM
Keep out unless you want
Something nasty to appen to you

Jane rummaged in her rucksack, pulled out a stethoscope and gave the wood a thorough check.

'We can't stop here, Fluffikins!' she said urgently. 'I do believe this is the secret storeroom that Mrs Brootle said we weren't to go near. We must get away!'

But just then my ears twitched, my whiskers pinged and my tail shot up in the air. It could mean only one thing – a call from The Snout. Jane grabbed me by the scruff of the neck and nipped off to a quiet corner.

She twiddled the tag on my collar.

'Where are you, Blond?' snapped The Snout. 'It's 13.23 and I haven't heard so much as a sniff from you.'

'I'm outside the secret storeroom with the sign that says, "Keep Out Unless You Want Something Nasty To 'appen To You", sir,' Jane whispered in my left ear. 'But don't worry. Fluffikins and I are about to go …'

'... and have a good nose around inside,' said The Snout happily. 'Excellent work, Blond. I knew I could rely on you. Safe sniffing.'

'But, sir,' wailed Jane. 'My Choccomunch ...'

It was too late. The Snout had gone.

Jane gave me a pat on the head.

'I can see you want to be off, Fluffikins, but don't forget we're still on a mission. Now let me think. A door like this is sure to be almost impossible to open. What shall I use? The Hooter Lockpicker? The Hooter Woodweakener? No, I have just the thing. Something fast and silent. The Hooter Powerpounder!'

Jane took an innocent-looking tissue box out of her rucksack and ripped open the top. There was a rude noise, and a large drill and goggles appeared in her hand. She got to work immediately.

At 13.31 precisely, Jane put down
the drill.

'I was right, Fluffikins,' she said.
'This door is impossible to open.'
Then she spotted the key in the
keyhole. 'Ah ha!' she exclaimed. 'A
secret key. How clever. But not too
clever for Jane Blond!'

She grasped the key and turned it.
The door burst open and the
Schoolgirl Superspy disappeared
under an avalanche of sweets and
chocolate. I could see that we had
found the stolen sweets of Snifton.

'Who put these in here?' Jane spluttered crossly, as she tried to fight her way out. 'I could have been killed. Crushed to death under a pile of … wait a minute, Fluffikins. It's all sweets and chocolate – and that means one thing. I have found my Choccomunch!'

She carefully sorted through the evidence.

'Isn't it lucky,' said Jane, as she chewed happily, 'that Badboys Hall

has so much Choccomunch, when there's none to be had in Snifton.'

She unwrapped her seventh bar. 'Wait a minute,' she exclaimed, jumping to her feet. 'PC Truncheon said the Choccomunch had been stolen along with all the other sweets in the town. That means the thief must have emptied the shops, crept up here and hidden the loot in this handy, empty secret storeroom. We must tell the headmaster at once!'

Suddenly the ground shook and three huge figures stomped round the corner. Three fat faces peered down menacingly at us.

'What's going on here?' yelled Mrs Brootle. 'Who's making all the racket? You woke us up from our after-dinner snooze, isn't that right, ladies?'

'That's right, Mrs Brootle.'

'Listen, Blong, I told you not to go near the secret storeroom that has the notice, "Keep Out Unless You Want Something Nasty To 'appen To You".'

'But, Mrs Brootle,' said Jane, scooping up as much Choccomunch as she could carry, 'there is no time to lose. I must see the headmaster immediately!'

'Well, it's your lucky day then,' snarled Mrs Brootle, rubbing her huge hands together in glee, 'because that's just where you're going. Grab 'em, ladies!'

CHAPTER SIX

At 13.57 precisely Mrs Brootle was thumping on the door of Professor Villain's office.

'ENTER!' boomed the loudspeaker.

The dinner ladies lumbered in and threw us to the floor.

I could see straight away that this was no ordinary headmaster's office. There were three clues – a huge gold swivel chair with its back to us, a desk covered in switches and flashing lights and, on the wall, a row of faces you wouldn't want to meet on a dark night.

Slowly the gold swivel chair turned. And there sat the headmaster of Badboys Hall, Professor Villain himself. He was small, he was skinny and he reminded me of a weasel.

'Whom have we here?' asked the Professor, squinting nastily at us.

'The name's Blond,' said Jane, pulling off her overall with a flourish. 'Jane Blond.'

There was a stunned silence. The jaws of the dinner ladies dropped in astonishment.

'Jane Blond,' breathed Professor Villain. 'Top Schoolgirl Superspy! Delighted to meet you.'

'Your dinner ladies brought us here on my instructions,' said Jane. 'I have something very important to …'

'Don't listen to her, Professor,' interrupted Mrs Brootle. 'We caught her and Shorty here snooping – in the secret storeroom!'

'The secret storeroom with the sign that says, "Keep Out Unless You Want Something Nasty To 'appen To You"?' said the headmaster, frowning.

'The very same. So can we do something nasty to them, Professor?'

'All in good time, Brootle.' Professor Villain fixed Jane with his beady little eyes. 'It's not every day I have the top agent of NOSY in my grasp. I want to hear what the famous Miss Blond has to say for herself.'

'Thanks, Prof,' said Jane. 'I have been carrying out a thorough investigation of your school, with Fluffikins here, and thanks to my top spying skills I have discovered the stolen sweets of Snifton. They are in your secret storeroom. I have brought some to show you. Naturally I shall need them to eat … I mean as evidence!'

She piled the Choccomunch on Professor Villain's desk.

The headmaster burst into a fit of mad laughter.

'Of course the sweets are in my secret storeroom!' he shrieked. 'It is all part of my clever plan to be Master Criminal of the Year!'

He jumped up from his chair, skipped over to the pictures on the wall and lovingly patted an empty space at the end of the row. 'Soon my picture will hang here amongst the greatest baddies of the age. It was I who started this school to train wrongdoers to work for me and obey my every command. It is I who keep them all in order, thanks to my voice magnifier here. I'll show you.'

He spoke into a huge funnel that stood on his desk. 'CALLING ALL PUPILS. PROFESSOR VILLAIN SPEAKING. DROP EVERYTHING AND LISTEN.'

A crashing sound echoed round the school. Professor Villain gave a horrible chuckle. 'And it was I who had the sweets and chocolate stolen from Snifton.'

As usual, Jane's keen mind was working at top speed.

'So what you're trying to say is,' she said, 'it was you who had the sweets and chocolate stolen from Snifton.'

'Correct,' sneered Professor Villain. 'And look what I've done to the town!'

He picked up a remote control and pressed a button. A massive television screen burst into life. It was 14.09 and a special newsflash was showing Snifton High Street, full of sobbing children. A worried-looking reporter was speaking to the camera.

'This is Ivor Scoop,' he was saying.

'The town of Snifton has come to a standstill following the strange disappearance of its sweets and chocolate. Even the school has closed. Who has done this terrible thing?'

'Oh dear,' said Jane. 'Don't you think you'd better hand it all back before you get into trouble, Prof?'

'Certainly not!' scoffed Professor Villain. 'That's not what master criminals do! Master criminals laugh in the face of trouble. Now I must get on with my grand plan. But first I will dispose of you and your hairy little friend. And I have a fitting end for the great Jane Blond.' He rubbed his chin. 'I'll have you chopped up and fed to the crocodile!'

'Excuse me, Professor,' said Mrs Brootle, shuffling her feet in embarrassment, 'but we haven't got a sharp knife. Not since we tried to cut Mrs Mince's fairy cakes.'

'No matter – we'll chuck them in whole!'

'Erm, we haven't got the crocodile any more, either,' said Mrs Brootle nervously. 'Remember that curry you ordered with extra bite – well, that was him.'

'Ah, yes, and very good it was too. So, we need another plan.'

'Excuse me, Professor.'

'What is it, Brootle?'

Mrs Brootle whispered something in Professor Villain's ear. An evil smile spread over Professor Villain's face.

'An excellent suggestion,' he smirked. 'What are we waiting for? Off to the kitchen!'

CHAPTER SEVEN

I could see straight away that things were not looking good for Jane Blond and her sidekick.

There were three clues. We had been tied up with ropes, we had been tossed into Mrs Brootle's mashing machine on top of a pile of lumpy boiled potatoes, and we were staring at two nasty blades above our heads, which were waiting to turn us into tomorrow's school dinner.

At that moment Professor Villain's weaselly face appeared above the bowl of the masher.

'You and your sidekick are about to be turned into tomorrow's school dinner, Miss Blond,' he announced with glee. 'But first I will tell you my life story.'

'I love a good story!' said Jane, stretching out on the potatoes to listen.

This was clever of the Schoolgirl Superspy. Master criminals always have to tell their victims their life story, and Jane would keep the Professor talking while I got busy on our ropes. It's all in a day's work for a sidekick who is also a cat with sharp teeth.

'I've always wanted to be a master criminal,' said Professor Villain importantly, 'so over the years I hatched a most daring plan. I decided I would rob Snifton's biggest bank and everyone would know the name of Archibald Villain. One night I climbed in a dark window at the back of the bank and set off to empty the vault of all its money. But I was foiled in my attempt.'

'What a shame!' said Jane sympathetically.

'It still pains me to talk of it,' gulped Professor Villain, wiping away a tear. 'Here, read this.' He flapped a newspaper cutting over our heads.

OH DEAR, WHAT CAN THE MATTER BE? SNIFTON MAN GETS LOCKED IN THE LAVATORY

Great drama unfolded yesterday at the Snifton Savings Bank in the High Street. At opening time, bank employees heard feeble knocking coming from the ladies' lavatory. Upon unlocking the door they found one of their customers, Mr Archivolt Willing, who had been mistakenly locked in. 'Every time I tried to climb out my foot slipped down the toilet,' sobbed a distraught Mr Willing, age 44. Bob Brass, the bank manager, issued a statement of apology and gave Mr Willing a gold-plated chequebook and pen.

'They didn't even spell my name right!' wailed Professor Villain, tucking the paper into his jacket pocket. 'I told them I was there to rob the bank, but they wouldn't listen.'

'How dreadful!' said Jane.

By now I had munched halfway through the ropes.

'From that day I vowed I would become the nastiest criminal Snifton had ever seen. And how better than by stealing their sweets and chocolate! So now I'm off to town to tell everyone it was I, Archibald Villain the Arch Villain, who was behind it all. And unless the people of Snifton do as I say, they will never see their confectionary again.

'I will rule the town – and I'm not stopping there. Today Snifton, tomorrow the world! Nothing can stop me being Master Criminal of the Year.'

Jane sighed.

'That was a lovely story, Prof,' she said. 'But I think you ought to give back all the sweets and chocolate now like a good boy.'

'I don't want to be a good boy!' shrieked the Professor. 'I want to be a master criminal! And that's what I'm going to be. Well, must dash. It's nearly half past two and I intend to appear on the three o'clock news. Goodbye, Miss Blond.'

The Professor disappeared and the kitchen door slammed. We heard Mrs Brootle give a nasty chuckle.

'You know what you have to do, Mrs Suett.'

'Yes, Mrs Brootle.'

There was the clunk of a switch as the potato masher was turned on. And, with a dreadful grinding noise, the blades above our heads started to rotate, slowly at first and then faster and faster. Then, to our horror, we saw them coming towards us. In five seconds flat we would be mashed to a pulp.

'There's no time to lose,' declared Jane. 'My trusty Hooter Laserblaster will stop this machine in its tracks. But first I must free myself. Ropes like these will be almost impossible to untie.'

With one tug the gnawed ropes fell away and Jane sat up. 'Hmm. Clever knots. But not too clever for Jane Blond.'

She whipped the spoon out from her rucksack, pointed it at the blades and tapped it three times. Nothing happened. She tapped the spoon again. Nothing. All the time the blades were getting closer. She thumped the side of the bowl with it. There was still no flash of blue light. It was obvious what was wrong. This was no Hooter Laserblaster. This was a custard spoon. Jane had taken the wrong one when we did the washing up!

'The Hooter Laserblaster doesn't seem to be working,' said Jane thoughtfully. 'Now this puts us in rather a pickle.'

The blades were almost upon us. It looked as if the Schoolgirl Superspy and her handy sidekick were done for!

CHAPTER EIGHT

I don't know how it happened, but the next minute Jane's wooden spoon was sailing through the air.

It whirled up, spun three times round the top of the mashing machine and dived into the spinning blades. There was a sickening crunch and the blades came to a mangled stop – centimetres from our noses.

'I knew the Hooter Laserblaster would do the trick,' muttered Jane.

'That was quick, wasn't it, ladies,' came Mrs Brootle's surprised voice.

'Yes, Mrs Brootle.'

'Shame there wasn't any screaming. Oh well, better scrape 'em out. Get the blades out of the way, Mrs Mince.'

'Yes, Mrs Brootle.'

Slowly the twisted blades began to move upwards. Quick as a flash we scrambled to our feet, leapt in the air and grabbed hold of the mangled mashers. As they rose out of the bowl, we rose with them, clutching as many boiled potatoes as we could.

There below were the dinner ladies, and they didn't look pleased to see us. They raised their ladles ready to attack. So we let them have it. Did we use the Hooterwhammer? Did we use the Hootershooter?

No, we splattered them with spuds.

By 14.53 Mrs Brootle, Mrs Mince and Mrs Suett were flat on their backs, covered in potatoes. They looked like a giant shepherd's pie.

They wouldn't be going anywhere for a while. And that suited us. We had a mission to complete. We had to stop Professor Villain before he appeared on television. We had seven minutes to save Snifton.

'We have a mission to complete,' said Jane. 'Follow me, Fluffikins.'

As soon as we were out of the kitchen Jane flattened herself on the floor and slithered along the corridor. I followed. We were making for the front door and the road to town.

By 14.55 we had reached the headmaster's office. Jane stopped and sniffed the air. Then she swerved expertly and slid in through the door. I knew what she was up to. The Schoolgirl Superspy was going to stop the Professor's evil plan – without even leaving Badboys Hall!

She scrambled up into the gold swivel chair and stuck her feet on the desk.

'Thank goodness my Choccomunch is still here,' she said, reaching for a bar. I could see why Jane was top agent for NOSY. There were five minutes to go until Snifton was taken over by a master criminal and she was as cool as a cucumber.

'As soon as I've finished my little snack, Fluffikins,' she said as she munched away, 'we shall ...'

I don't know how it happened but somehow all the pupils of Badboys Hall heard what she said next.

'... GET ALL THE SWEETS AND CHOCOLATE FROM THE SECRET STOREROOM AND TAKE THEM BACK TO THE CHILDREN OF SNIFTON.'

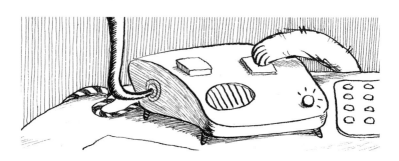

Her words echoed round the school. Immediately there was a thunder of running feet, a rustling of sweets and a slamming of doors.

Jane reached for another bar of Choccomunch and the television control.

At 15.00 on the dot she flicked a switch and Professor Villain immediately appeared on the huge screen. Behind him stood the howling children of Snifton and beside him Ivor Scoop was talking excitedly into a microphone.

'I am here with Professor Archibald Villain, headmaster of Badboys Hall Primary School, who says he can clear up this terrible mystery.'

Professor Villain puffed out his chest and smirked at the camera.

'Listen to me, you snivelling citizens of Snifton,' he sneered into the microphone. 'This was all my doing. It was I who took all the sweets and chocolate and ...'

He stopped as a commotion broke out behind him. The pupils of Badboys Hall were marching up the High Street, throwing handfuls of sweets and chocolate to the cheering children.

Ivor Scoop broke in '... and you are having them handed out to all the kids of the town. You are a good, kind man.'

'No, I'm not!' screamed Professor Villain, going purple with rage. 'I am Archibald Villain the Arch Villain! I'm bad. I'm evil. I'm the worst criminal the world has ever known! Who has ruined my master plan? Someone is going to pay for this.'

'And you, the good people of Snifton, heard it here first,' interrupted the reporter. 'This hero of a headmaster is going to pay for all the sweets!'

Jane flicked the television off.

'There you are, Fluffikins,' she said, 'I knew Professor Villain would listen to my advice and give the sweets and chocolate back. After all, Schoolgirl Superspies are always right.'

She grabbed me by the scruff of the neck and swept me off to a quiet corner underneath the picture of Cuthbert Clod, Master Criminal of the Year 1995.

She twiddled the tag on my collar. My ears twitched, my whiskers pinged and my tail shot up in the air. 'Blond calling,' Jane whispered into my left ear. 'Jane Blond. Mission completed, sir.'

'I know, Blond,' came The Snout's voice. 'I've just seen it on the television. Congratulations on solving the mystery of Badboys Hall! But there's no rest for the top agent of NOSY. I have another job for you.'

'Fire away, sir.'

'I want you to go straight to the library and seek out Mr Hooter. Then …'

'Ready and waiting, sir.'

'… I want you to renew my library books. Safe sniffing.'

CHAPTER NINE

The next morning we were in Mr Sherbet's shop. It was 07.54, the shopkeeper was beaming and the shelves were brimming with sweets and chocolate. As Jane filled her Schoolgirl Superspy rucksack with Choccomunch, a headline in the local paper caught my eye. I sauntered over to have a quick read.

SWEETS FOUND SAFE AND SOUND
HERO HEADMASTER SAVES SNIFTON FROM DISASTER

A local headmaster saved the day yesterday by finding the famous missing sweets and chocolate of Snifton. But kindly Professor Artichoke Filling of Badboys Hall Primary School didn't stop there. Instead of taking it back to the shops he gave it all to the children and paid the shopkeepers out of his own pocket. So everybody is happy in Snifton.

Somehow I didn't think the Professor would be feeling very pleased with himself.

Jane paid Mr Sherbet and hoisted her rucksack on to her back.

'Come on, Fluffikins,' she called as she staggered towards the door. 'We can't stand around here all day.'

Then she saw Professor Villain's photo glaring out from the paper.

'Oh look!' she said. 'There's Professor Villain. I expect he's feeling really pleased with himself. The whole of Snifton loves him. But I don't suppose you remember him, do you, Fluffikins. After all, you're only a cat.'

So now you know the truth about the story of Jane Blond and the Missing Chocolate. Don't forget, this is top secret information. Only you know how the top agent from NOSY overcame a dastardly criminal and saved Snifton – with a little help from her sidekick. You must tell no one what you have read – not even your best friend.

And now listen very carefully. I want you to do three things:

1. Slowly close this book.

2. Put it down somewhere safe.

3. RUN FOR YOUR LIFE!

This book will self-destruct in precisely ten seconds
   … nine
      … eight
         … seven
            … six